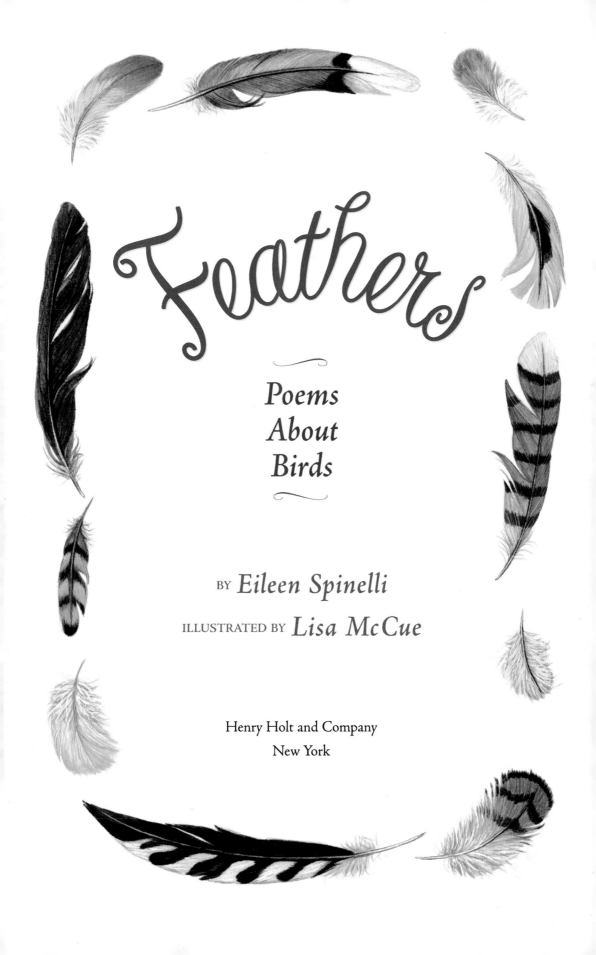

Feathers

Poems About Birds

BY Eileen Spinelli

ILLUSTRATED BY Lisa McCue

Henry Holt and Company
New York

For my book friends Frank Hodge and Dan Darigan,
who make children's literature take wing
—E. S.

To all the bird lovers who helped me bring these beautiful birds to life—
with a special thanks to Katherine Haas, Ken and Bee Karsten,
Martin Beadle, Ann Swanson, and with fond remembrance of Cheek
—L. M.

Contents

No rooster to wake us.
We're not on a farm.
But we have our very own
feathered alarm.
It drums before breakfast
on shingle and pole.
I think there's some rooster
in woodpecker's soul.

GREETINGS

How do pelicans say hello
when meeting on the beach below?
They puff out their pouches,
point beaks to the sky.
They turn their heads
from side to side.
That's how pelicans say hello!
So now you know.

Show Bird

Blue-footed booby,
do be a dear—
do high-step your blue feet.
Do dive off the pier.
Do show off your skills
as a catcher of fish.
Do whistle.
Do waddle.
Then—
do what you wish.

NEEDLE BEAK

Silk from a spider,
string (sometimes red),
grass from a meadow—
all make the thread
that tailorbird
stitches
into a bed.

Guess Which Bird This Is

Dizzy-dazzle thrumming bird.
No bigger-than-my-thumb-ing bird.
A silky, summer-strumming bird.
A going-and-a-coming bird.

(The answer is: the hummingbird.)

WATER·WINGS

On their
flippery
dippery
wings
penguins fly
through
watersky.

THOSE SOCIABLE WEAVERS

Using grass and leaves and twigs,
weaverbirds build fancy digs—
a common roof, with knots and laces
tied to separate condo spaces.

Weaverbirds are generous, kind.
For instance, they don't seem to mind
if parrot, favoring the view,
occupies a room or two.

DON'T EVEN ASK

The stately secretary bird
won't sort your mail,
won't type a word.
Won't take your coat.
Won't hang your hat.
Won't answer phones.
And that
is that.

Goldfinch

Soaring up.
Swooping down.
Hooping happy
round and round.
Looping is
the flight preferred
by this roller-coaster bird.

THE WADING
BIRD OF EGYPT

Plover wades the river Nile.
Rides the back of crocodile.
Brave, bold plover!

Hungry plover's even bolder.
Steps on crocodile's shoulder.
Down the snout
and in the mouth
of the croc who's swimming south.
Rash, brash plover!

Plover picks crocodile's teeth—
row on top,
row beneath.
Dining done,
he straggles out,
none the worse for wear,
no doubt.
Plucky,
lucky plover.

Water Sprite

The dipper splashes, swims, and sprays.
In waterfalls it spends its days.
I wonder—if this bird could wish,
would it prefer to be a fish?

HoMeLess

Fairy tern borrows
the branch of a tree.
She lays her egg
at the edge—
carefully!
Then when her chick hatches
it scritches, it scratches
and tries not to fall
from its no-nest-at-all.

TOUCANANTICS

Playful toucan
plucks a berry,
tosses it
to toucan two.
Toucan two
looks for another
toucan he can
toss it to.
Toucan three
is free
to toss it
to a fourth
or back to one
or . . .
he can decide to eat it.
Game done!

THIRSTY

Cedar waxwing,
you catch snowflakes
as they fall.
I like to catch
snowflakes too—
feel them melting
on my tongue—
just like you,
cedar waxwing.

Some Games Are for the Birds

Skip and scamper.
Hop and run.
Chasing chickadee
is fun.
Not so fun
is chickadee
turned around
and chasing me!

SHREWD

Elf owl watches
poor woodpecker work
pecking a hole in saguaro.
Not one bit embarrassed
at being a shirker,
she'll make it *her* nest
by tomorrow!

THE CHASE

Roadrunner can fly
when it cares to.
Roadrunner can fly
when it dares to.
But it most likes to run
in the bright desert sun
so, lizard, beware—
it might snare you!

Country Bumpkin

Crow swoops in
one early morn.
Nips the berries.
Eats the corn.
Pecks the pumpkins—
rat-a-tat.
Naps on scarecrow's
rumpled hat.
Like the farmer
and his wife,
crow prefers
the country life.

Spring Real Estate

Here is a house, dear robin.
The floor and walls are strong.
It's safe from wind
and snug from rain
and yours for just a song.

27

WHAT'S THAT SOUND?

A scraping chair,
a whistling train,
a fire bell,
an aeroplane,
a clock alarm,
a fence of crows,
a goose, a gong,
a blowing nose . . .
Australian lyrebird
can sing
to sound like
almost anything.

SWEET TOOTH

Care for honey with your tea?
Grab a spoon and follow me,
chat-a-chatters honeyguide.
I know where the bees reside—
south a ways
then toward the east.
I can lead you to a feast!

Courtship

Bowerbird sings to his lady love:
Now see what I have made for you—
a courting nest with leaves and flowers,
with tiny shells and stones of blue,
with lacy fern and foil wraps
and seven shiny bottle caps.
I found a brush of tender bark
and berry juice to paint inside.
I found a ribbon, soft and wide.
Come, lady love, and be my bride.

By nature
peacock's rather prone
to wanting to be
left alone.

Alas, his tail
does not agree.
It calls to all:
Come look at me!

BABY SWAN

When a cygnet is tired
or frightened,
when a cygnet is cold,
then it clings
to the feathery back
of its mother,
who cuddles it
under her wings
(with love),
who cradles it
under her wings.

EXTENDED FAMILY

Chimney swifts,
in nasty weather,
roost in a huddle
and cuddle together.
Hail down, ye ice,
or rail, ye storm—
chimney swifts
keep cozy, warm.

CHANGE

Once called rock doves,
pigeons flew
to rugged cliffs
of silver hue
and gazed on rivers
winding through.

Now pigeons fly
across the sky to city buildings
rising high
and watch the taxis
scuttle by.

Nighty-Night

Soon after sunset
nighthawk flies
toward the city's
bright-lit skies,
its wings a flight of
lullabies.

Some Feathery Facts

The WOODPECKER uses its long bill for drilling holes in trees. In this way it finds food (insects) and makes a nest. Most males have red feathers on their heads. Woodpeckers live in almost all parts of the world.

A ROOSTER is a male chicken. It does not lay eggs or help raise the chicks. The rooster is famous for crowing in the morning, but it also crows at other times.

The PELICAN is a seabird. It stores fish in a pouch below its bill. This bird is a strong swimmer and flier, but it's clumsy on land.

The BLUE-FOOTED BOOBY is a tropical seabird about the size of a goose. And yes, its feet are—amazingly—bright blue!

The TAILORBIRD is a songbird found in tropical regions throughout southeast Asia. It uses its bill as a needle, darning leaves together with cotton fibers, spiderweb silk, and other natural threads.

The smallest bird in the world is the HUMMINGBIRD. It can hover like a helicopter in midair. It can also fly backward. The humming sound of the bird's wings is what gives it its name.

Though the PENGUIN is a bird, it cannot fly. But it's good at swimming and diving. A penguin's wings are like flippers. Its favorite food is fish.

The WEAVERBIRD is good at cooperating. As many as 150 weaverbirds will work together to build a huge nest of grass and twigs high in a tree.

The SECRETARY BIRD is one of the world's largest birds of prey. It lives in the grasslands of tropical Africa. This bird can run faster than a human. At night it sleeps in a tree.

The GOLDFINCH is sometimes called the wild canary because of its yellow color and pretty song. The male goldfinch feeds the female while she sits on the eggs, and he provides most of the food for the chicks.

The EGYPTIAN PLOVER prefers rivers to lakes or ponds. It does not like thick forest areas. The plover doesn't seem to be afraid of people.

The DIPPER can walk underwater. It has stubby wings and a short tail. Some dippers build nests of moss behind waterfalls.

The FAIRY TERN is a seabird related to the gull. It makes no nest but lays its single egg in a hollow place on a branch or rock ledge. A parent sits on the egg until it hatches.

The TOUCAN lives in the tropical forests of South and Central America. It has an enormous bill. The bill of a toucan may be black, blue, green, red, white, yellow, or a combination of colors. There are about forty kinds of toucans.

The CEDAR WAXWING is named for the red tips of its wing feathers. These feathers look like the wax used long ago to seal letters. The cedar waxwing feeds mostly on berries. It is also fond of maple sap.

The CHICKADEE is a small, acrobatic bird. It eats berries, seeds, nuts, fruits, and bugs. On winter nights chickadees keep warm by roosting together in old nests.

The smallest owl in the world is the ELF OWL. It is only six inches long. The elf owl makes its home in an empty hole in the saguaro cactus.

The ROADRUNNER can fly. And it will—to escape danger. But it much prefers running zigzag across the deserts of the southwest United States.

The CROW is a large black bird. When a crow eats a farmer's corn or wheat, the farmer isn't happy. But when a crow eats the insects that damage the farmer's crops—well—that's another story.

The AMERICAN ROBIN is one of the first birds to return north in the spring. The male has a brick-red breast. The female is slightly smaller. She is also duller in color.

One of the most unusual Australian birds is the LYREBIRD. Its large spreading tail feathers are arranged like an ancient lyre. This bird has a melodious song. It can also imitate other birds and sounds.

The HONEYGUIDE is found in tropical Africa and Asia. It guides animals and people to beehives. The animals and people eat the honey. The honeyguide eats the beeswax.

The BOWERBIRD is named for its "bower," an area prettily decorated by the male. Here is where he bows and dances and courts his mate. Some bowerbirds have bright plumage. Others are rather plain.

The PEACOCK is a member of the pheasant family. It has splendid feathers that spread out into a fan. These feathers are called a train.

A CYGNET is a baby swan. It looks nothing like its beautiful parents. A cygnet is fuzzy and gray. Of course, mother swan loves it anyway.

The CHIMNEY SWIFT is sooty gray. It spends most of its time in the air. It feeds in the air. Some observers believe it even sleeps in the air. Sometimes a flock of chimney swifts will use a chimney as a resting post.

The PIGEON is common in most cities. It is swift and powerful. Homing pigeons are used for carrying messages and for racing. Most pigeons live in flocks.

The NIGHTHAWK is not a hawk at all. It is related to the whippoorwill. As soon as the sun sets, the nighthawk flies to look for insects. It winters in South America.

Henry Holt and Company, LLC
Publishers since 1866
115 West 18th Street
New York, New York 10011
www.henryholt.com

Henry Holt is a registered trademark of Henry Holt and Company, LLC
Text copyright © 2004 by Eileen Spinelli
Illustrations copyright © 2004 by Lisa McCue
All rights reserved.
Distributed in Canada by H. B. Fenn and Company Ltd.

Library of Congress Cataloging-in-Publication Data
Spinelli, Eileen.
Feathers: poems about birds / by Eileen Spinelli; illustrated by Lisa McCue.
p.   cm.
Summary: More than twenty-five poems about both common and unusual birds.
1. Birds—Juvenile poetry. 2. Children's poetry, American. [1. Birds—Poetry. 2. American poetry.]
I. McCue, Lisa, ill. II. Title.
PS3569.P5457F43 2004   811'.54—dc21   2003002620

ISBN 0-8050-6713-2
First Edition—2004
Printed in the United States of America on acid-free paper. ∞

1 3 5 7 9 10 8 6 4 2

The artist used watercolors and acrylics on Arches watercolor paper
to create the illustrations for this book.

The poems "Country Bumpkin" and "Spring Real Estate" were originally published
in *On the Line* magazine.